A NOTE TO PARENTS

Reading Aloud with Your Child

Research shows that reading books most valuable support parents can children learn to read.

- Be a ham! The more enthusiasm you display, the your child will enjoy the book.
- Run your finger underneath the words as you read to signal that the print carries the story.
- Leave time for examining the illustrations more closely; encourage your child to find things in the pictures.
- Invite your youngster to join in whenever there's a repeated phrase in the text.
- Link up events in the book with similar events in your child's life.
- If your child asks a question, stop and answer it. The book can be a means to learning more about your child's thoughts.

Listening to Your Child Read Aloud

The support of your attention and praise is absolutely crucial to your child's continuing efforts to learn to read.

- If your child is learning to read and asks for a word, give it immediately so that the meaning of the story is not interrupted. DO NOT ask your child to sound out the word.
- On the other hand, if your child initiates the act of sounding out, don't intervene.
- If your child is reading along and makes what is called a miscue, listen for the sense of the miscue. If the word "road" is substituted for the word "street," for instance, no meaning is lost. Don't stop the reading for a correction.
- If the miscue makes no sense (for example, "horse" for "house"), ask your child to reread the sentence because you're not sure you understand what's just been read.
- Above all else, enjoy your child's growing command of print and make sure you give lots of praise. *You are your child's first teacher — and the most important one. Praise from you is critical for further risk-taking and learning.*

— Priscilla Lynch
Ph.D., New York University
Educational Consultant

Library of Congress Cataloging-in-Publication Data

Wilhelm, Hans, 1945-
        I hate my bow! / by Hans Wilhelm.
        p.   cm. — (Hello reader! Level 1)
    Summary: A little dog laments the fact that the other dogs won't play with
        him as long as he has a bath, a bow, and a chain.
    ISBN 0-590-25519-3
    [1. Dogs—Fiction.   2. Play—Fiction.]   I. Title.   II. Series:
    Hello reader! Level 1.
PZ7.W64816Iah   1995   94-37431
[E]—dc20   CIP
                                                               AC

12 11 10 9 8 7 6 5 4 3 2   5 6 7 8 9/9 0/0

Printed in the U.S.A.   23

First Scholastic printing, April 1995

I HATE MY BOW!

by Hans Wilhelm

Hello Reader! — Level 1

SCHOLASTIC INC.
New York Toronto London Auckland Sydney

I hate my bath.

I hate my bow.

I hate my chain.

I hate this baby.

I hate this cat.

Hi, guys. May I play with you?

Oops!

Those guys won't play
with a dog
with a bath
and a bow
and a chain.

I have an idea.

Come here, cat.

Take the pretty bow.

Come here, baby.

Take the pretty chain.

Now let's play in the mud.

I love my new friends.